MW01596066

A NOVELLA-IN-FLASH
BY KIEREN WESTWOOD

Shortlisted for the Bath Novella-in-Flash Award 2020.

GOLD
FURY

For Hayley

One

A long, empty road, flat fields either side. It could have been winter, or summer, or the surface of mars. A man stood with his arm extended over the white line. He was still enough to be a scarecrow and about as weather-beaten.

Forty-four cars passed by staring, before a gold 1970 Plymouth Fury blinked and floated to the side of the road like a docking cruise ship.

The scarecrow bent to pick up his duffel bag and held the revolver behind it, checking first that it was loaded, though he knew it was. Eyeing the Fury's driver, he limped over and put his hand on the roof directly above the driver's head. The window came down inch by inch.

'Where you hoping to go?' A friendly voice came from the driver's seat. The scarecrow looked down at his feet, where a wasp was crawling through the dust towards his boot.

The scarecrow leaned down. 'Why?'

'Well, I might not be going the same place as you is all.'

'You're not.'

'I'm not? Well how d'you know that if I ain't said where I'm going yet?'

The driver frowned, or shrugged, or looked worried. The scarecrow had never been too good on faces. This was before the gun came out. When it did, the driver's face was stuck fast, wide eyed. He gasped for one big breath as though about to be submerged in water.

The scarecrow reached in and pulled the door release, keeping the revolver held just inside the car, hidden from the highway, if anyone dared to pass.

'Okay, okay…' the driver said. He didn't look at the scarecrow. People often didn't.

'I just need…Let me get my papers from…'

The scarecrow fired over the roof of the car, out into the fields. Smell of burning and sweat.

'OK, OK, OK.'

The driver slid from the seat and seemed to have trouble standing. The scarecrow squashed him in the open door and leaned his face close.

'If I see you turn...' he sang in a low register, trailing off. He watched the driver's eyes and pressed down for a few seconds, then let go. The driver stumbled and took off into the empty field, leaving a wake of dust. The scarecrow watched him go for a while, before throwing his bag in the back. By the time the next car passed, the driver had almost made the tree line and hadn't looked back.

The scarecrow opened the glove compartment and rammed the gun into it, atop a load of papers he didn't bother looking at, and forced it shut.

He swung the car around and gunned it back the way it came. The radio worked. He turned it up as loud as it would go and he drove.

He lost the light before he made it all that far.

Three times he floated onto the rumble strips and three times he course-corrected. The fourth time, he just let it keep going and found himself parked in a field as the evening rolled over him like a wave of gas. He spent that night with the windows down listening to the breeze snaking through the grass. The gun in the glove compartment felt like a part of himself, nestled among the papers. Even locked away he felt its sights resting on him. Saw it in his mind, imagined it firing of its own accord.

He woke in the night when something bounced off the roof, heavy and small. The only recourse he had was to lean out of the window and stare up at the rash of stars. He shouted into the cosmos for it to keep its shit to itself. His bottle tumbled out of the window into the long grass and he passed out again slumped over the door, talking to his father, or himself.

Two

A hammering on the plank door the like to bring the whole cabin down. The day rushed Reid and surrounded him like an ambush. He'd seen this day coming and he just couldn't get out of the way.

'God damn, kid,' he said, to help him get upright.

Hammering again, longer.

'I'm coming, save the wood for Chrissakes.' He dragged himself up out of bed and resolved to cough his way to the door.

The kid was there, retreated now to the bottom of the steps, out of swinging range. He had a look in his eye like something was happening and he was going to make the most of it.

'Someone's on our land again,' the kid said.

'My land. What time is it?'

'It's past dawn. Someone's on-'

'You said that. I thought you were camping?'

'I was coming back.'

'This early? How much of my woods did you burn down exactly?'

'I didn't burn anything, I...'

'I what?'

'I needed the bathroom.'

He rolled his eyes at the kid and headed down the stairs and into the yard.

Of all the days for this to happen, there was a sad old joke here. He was going to turf someone off his land for the last time, before he got turfed off it himself. Now the boy was back to see it all happen, all because he needed to take a dump. What kind of teenager couldn't get lost in the woods, even for a day? Reid had never even seen him with a friend around. Not one time.

'Where am I going, exactly?' Reid said. His breath wheezed out like stale air from a punctured tire.

'The west field, by the highway, the one with the big stump in the middle.'

'And who's there?' They set off walking. It was a quarter of a mile, plenty of time to get back to the farm before they came but not a lot of reason to. No need to rush his bad legs.

'A guy in a car, he looked sick or something.'

'Sick? You mean drunk?'

The kid shrugged. 'I'm not a doctor.'

Reid just gave him a look and pointed to his smart mouth.

'In a car you said? What, he parked by the road and pitched up a tent?'

'No, he was in his car, in the field,' the kid said. Reid said nothing to that, but picked up the pace as much as he could.

They stood a few minutes by the gate, looking at the car.

'An old Fury by the looks of it.'

'Yeah,' the kid said it like he knew.

'Where were you camped?'

He pointed into the trees some way off.

'You hear him come in the night?'

The kid shook his head. 'I didn't go near him.'

'Sure you didn't.'

Reid saw as he got closer that the guy was long gone, the grass was beat down in a wavy line towards the highway.

He stood for a moment, feeling the dew on his legs and a cool wind behind him. Some way off, birds were singing. They sounded nervous, like they were in an audition and none too sure they should be.

There would be no steering the car out, it was bogged in the mud. He leaned in and smelled drink, old cigarettes. All the windows were down. The glove compartment was open and there were letters spilling out, one of them still sealed. Not his business, he crossed to the other side and collected them, put them back.

'What's that?' the kid said, trying to work his way between Reid and the passenger seat.

'Nothing, get out of there.'

Reid straightened up and looked to the highway, still empty.

On the roof of the car, a fist sized rock sat next to a good-sized dent.

I didn't go near him. Right.

'Kid,' he said. He leaned on the car and closed his eyes until the pain in his legs eased.

The boy appeared again from somewhere and Reid turned to him.

'Run back to the cabin, call Helen or whoever's there, tell them I need a winch at the west field.'

The kid nodded like he was glad of a mission.

'Alright, now say that back to me.'

He watched the kid go and stayed leaning on the car. Off down the highway, he saw the ghosts of cars making their way towards everything he had built. Coming for him. Letters in their glove compartments too. His business.

Three

'Shall I pull over?' she said. She grinned and nodded towards the side of the road.

'What? No. What's wrong with you?'

'It was a joke Denny. Christ.'

'He looks like he spent the night digging out of his own grave, look at him.'

Helen rolled her eyes and watched the figure with his arm out get smaller in the mirror. He'd turned to follow their progress down the road as though to pass him had been a betrayal. His arm had fallen and she saw his breath leave him like a mushroom cloud.

She shook the feeling off, trying to remember what had seemed funny a few moments before.

Three years and she was still trying to joke with a man with no sense of humour.

Reid's farm was a few miles outside of town, the drive passed slowly, mostly in silence. Helen tried her best to break it where she could.

'Look at that guy,' she said, taking one hand off the wheel to point at a billboard at the side of the highway. 'Would you trust him for Governor?'

'Who?' Denny said, irritated, looking up from his phone.

Helen pointed at the billboard again as they passed it. A plastic-smiling man in a rigid looking suit stared at them as they passed. The smile seemed to become a grimace the closer they got.

'John Mandle for Governor, that's who,' Helen said. 'Looks shady to me. He's crooked as a witch's nose right? What do you think?'

Denny shrugged. 'Heard he's got it in for illegals.'

'That's putting it lightly, way I've heard it told,' Helen said. Denny didn't reply but that was fine. She didn't know whether Denny was supporting or opposing that particular stance and she didn't want to know either. She gave up talking.

'Is this it?' she said, another mile down the road. The hedge was beaten down and there were tire marks on the old asphalt.

'I don't know, maybe.'

'Gee thanks.'

She slowed down and signaled, there was a truck some way behind but she thought she'd be clear before it got to them, she didn't want to make it have to slow any.

Level with the gap in the fence, she made a half turn and reversed off the road and down the bank, leaning out to navigate. Denny scrolled through his phone.

'That about right, you think?'

'Mmm,' he said, without looking up.

'Great.' She put the lights on and got out and slammed the door with everything she had, leaving him to sit there in the aftermath of it, probably swearing.

Reid was leaning up on the car when she got to him.

'Morning. What happened?'

'The hell if I know, my grandson found it this morning. There was a driver then. Now there ain't. Got these though.' He held up the keys.

'Ah, easy. I'll get the winch.' She set off towards the truck but turned back. 'You alright Reid?'

'Just my legs, nothing I can't handle.'

She nodded and followed the tire tracks through the grass, almost to the truck, where she stood on the running board and slapped Denny's window.

He opened his door. 'Jesus Christ, what?!'

'Reid's got the keys.'

Denny rolled his eyes and slumped out. She got in and let the winch loose and watched him attach it in the wing mirror, saw the rear lights of the old Fury come on.

Denny got back in and slammed the door behind him.

'Secure?' Helen said.

'Yeah.'

'Did you-'

'Yes goddamn it, I double checked everything.'

'It wouldn't be the first time, that's all I'm saying.'

Denny looked at her the same way he looked at any work that was coming his way, then he turned and stared out of the window across the fields.

Helen could hear the old car rattling as they doubled back on the highway.

When they got close to town, Denny saw fit to start talking again.

'There's a bunch of crap in there.'

'In where?'

'Umm, the car?' he scoffed. 'Bunch of letters and shit. Stinks in there too.'

Helen frowned.

'Was there gas in it when you started it up?'

'A quarter tank, yeah.'

'And stuff in there, personal effects?'

'Letters yeah, I said that.'

Helen signaled and turned around in a wide, fast arc over the empty road. Denny gripped his seatbelt. She rode the curb for a just a second. The gold Fury riding on their back sounded like a great metal piano being dropped.

'The fuck are you doing?'

'We're taking it to Letwin.'

'Him? Again?' Denny said.

Four

Letwin heard the truck pull in and sit idling outside, but he stayed where he was, looking at the framed picture of one of the great lakes lying on the floor where it must have fallen in the night. The office was a mess. He'd have to think about a cleaner, or do it himself if it wasn't in the budget. He tried not to look at the photograph next to his monitor. The three of them at Magic Kingdom. He closed his eyes.

After a few minutes, Oliver poked his head around the door.

'Chief, Helen's got a wrecker here, bit of a strange one.'

Letwin took a breath and followed him outside, catching the door just before it closed on him. There was time to gather his thoughts and be professional, he'd need to be, especially if she'd brought Denny. The guy was none too smart, but lying is lying and some people can spot it.

They were gathered around the truck looking up at a Plymouth Fury, gold in colour and rusted under the wheel arches. Letwin nodded to them without saying anything at first. He circled the car, no impact, it looked old and dirty but still whole.

'Shut the engine off,' Helen said.

'What you got Helen?' he finally said. He looked her in the eye and felt it jolt through him. Tried to ignore the shadow of a smile she was wearing.

'Just thought it was odd, Chief,' she called him that like it was a joke just between them. 'Reid called it in, it came off the road yesterday sometime he thinks, he found it like that. His grandson said there was someone in it, but they were nowhere to be seen, so…'

'I can't see why he'd lie,' Letwin said, scratching an itch on his cheek. He reached up and ran his hand over the front fender, not really knowing what he was looking for. A pulse, a static charge, something. 'Empty?'

'That's the thing,' Helen said. 'It's got a quarter tank and Denny started it straight up, nothing wrong with it other than it was bogged in. It took out a few feet of Reid's hedge but no mechanical damage. Why would they leave it?'

Letwin had a few ideas but he kept them to himself. He took his notebook out and wrote the licence down, hauled himself onto the back of the truck.

'Give him the keys Denny.'

Denny rolled his eyes and fished the keys from some dark pocket. Letwin caught them one-handed against his chest and opened the driver's door. He brushed dust off the metal plate so he could read the VIN.

There were empty bottles and cigarette stubs in the front, rags in the back. He jumped down, then pushed the door closed.

'Alright, well. Probably best we keep hold of it. Someone might want to claim it. Could be that they went looking for something, aiming to come back. If they can't find it, maybe they'll come knocking at my door.'

'Where do you want it?'

'Ideally, over at the lot, but-'

'That lot?' Denny said, pointing.

'That's McDonalds, dummy,' Helen said, 'he means the impound.'

'Ah Christ. We gotta-'

'You got time?' Letwin cut across him, talking to Helen. The spark came back and the sentence seemed to wear a disguise, though he hadn't meant it to. She smiled what could have been simple politeness, but wasn't.

'Sure. We've got to go back to Reid's shortly, but we should have time.'

'What else does Reid need a winch for?' Letwin asked.

'Yeah,' Denny said smirking, 'his old lady's been dead these two years now.' He started laughing. No one else did.

'You're a real asshole Denny,' Helen said, quiet.

Letwin stared as hard as he could at Denny, until the man looked away.

'Thanks for bringing it in. I'd better get back to it, if you'll excuse me,' Letwin said. Helen didn't meet his eyes. Denny had already gone back to the truck but she lingered a moment before following him.

'Be careful at the lot, they've had some trouble the past couple of weeks,' Letwin said so no one else would hear.

She nodded at the ground.

'Something don't add up there, huh?' Oliver said as they watched the truck pull out onto the road.

Letwin thought about asking him exactly what he meant.

Five

They had to keep the lights off at night, except for a fluorescent bug light in the back room where the window was broken. They'd found it in one of the cars and it saved them getting eaten alive.

Randall was kneeling, prising the blinds apart with two fingers, watching the dark. Hoss had gone out three hours before. He'd left the back way, through the yard and into the woods so he wouldn't be seen, and he'd taken most of their tools.

It hadn't seemed like a big deal to Randall then. Hoss had never been gone more than an hour before but he just had a special important job like he said. They'd been squatting there for weeks with no problems, A-OK. Randall had behaved. Randall had been quiet, just like Hoss said. Hoss had barely got mad.

There was movement in the lot again, it pulled his thoughts back to what he could see. Car lights, bright ones. A man getting out, opening the gate, getting back in again and driving out.

Randall giggled to himself. He'd made up his mind an hour ago what he was going to do. Go to work and get them some stuff. Hoss would love him for it when he finally got back.

The lot had two new cars. Ones that he hadn't looked in yet. He'd watched them get dropped off on a truck with a hook.

'Truck with a hook,' Randall whispered into the dark.

He let the blinds close and looked at his pile of treasures in the corner of the room. One time someone's sitting room, probably. There was a wallet containing twenty different movie stubs, a corked glass bottle of something, a handheld machine he wasn't sure the workings of, endless items of clothing and litter. An ever-growing pile of tiny debris chips from people's lives.

Hoss had wanted to burn it all in the night. No, he did get mad, that was right. Only once though. He was scared they'd be found out, but the man in the impound didn't know anything. Not one thing. No one knew about Randall's treasures except for Randall and Hoss. No one missed them.

He watched the car lights turn from white to red and get smaller and smaller, then he waited, just like he was told. He listened to the crickets talk, and the wind passing through the holes in the house, whispering like Randall liked to do.

Time to move, move, move.

Giggling, he made sure his backpack was on both shoulders and crept out of the house, keeping ducked low.

They'd made a hole in the fence where it wouldn't be seen behind the skeleton of a big car that he thought used to be bright firetruck red. He caught his trousers where the fence was cut sharp and heard them rip. Stifling a snort of laughter, he pulled himself free and headed for the new cars.

The idiot who ran the place didn't have no cameras, no security, no systems at all, Hoss had said. You could walk right up and take what you wanted, long as no one saw.

Randall went straight for the gold one. He'd seen it on the back of the truck going in.

Truck with a hook, he thought to himself. Keeping it in his head like Hoss said to do.

Crouching in the mud beside the car he read the name on the front fender, *Fury,* and chuckled.

They'd left it open too, it was easy. Nothing much in the back, some more clothes. The back wasn't his favorite anyway. The hidey-hole in the front was. That's where folks put all the special stuff.

The passenger door creaked as he opened it, making him jump, then giggle. The hidey-hole was unlocked and the door fell open with a clunk. Papers fell out, loads of them, all covered in stories.

Lights went on all around him, blinding, hurting his eyes.

'Stay where you are, hands where we can see them,' someone said over a loudspeaker. He couldn't see them.

Then they were all around him, coming closer. Men with guns and hats and coats.

'Try something son,' someone else said, close by and quiet. Silhouette of a man with his hand at his hip.

Some of the letters fell to the floor.

Randall shouted for Hoss, but Hoss couldn't hear him.

Six

Oliver listened to the crackle on the line, the distance. Years ago he used to think it was birds on the wire, somewhere out in the dark. Now he knew better, but he still didn't know what it was.

He looked at his watch, turned it to catch the light. He'd got the time difference wrong but the phone was already ringing.

'Oliver,' a gruff voice said, not a question, a response.

'Yeah Harley, how did you know it was me?' His voice filled the lockup from corner to corner, checking to see if it was watertight. The fluorescent light above him flickered like he'd woken it up.

'Figured. It's gone midnight, who else would drag an old man out of bed?'

'Shit, did I?'

'No.'

Oliver rolled his eyes. But he needed the help.

'You got something?' the old man said.

'I think I have,' Oliver said. He ran his hand over the car. When he turned it over it was covered in dust from the road.

'The Chief know you're calling?'

'He's not interested, he never is.'

I said no, Oliver. It's just an abandoned old junker. We're pressed as it is, we don't have the cash to have it searched and processed and whatever else big plans you had for it. What if the owner shows up and we say, oh yeah sorry sir, we're just fingerprinting the entire car. It's not even stolen for sure. Leave it. Don't make me say it again. Give me the keys.

'Seems an odd duck, that Mr Letwin,' Harley said. Oliver could hear a chair being pulled out on the old man's side. He pictured the small kitchen, the good oak and smell of dogs. 'What you got?'

'We picked up a car, abandoned, yesterday, can't trace the owner. His wife says he's not been home for a couple of nights.'

'What kind?'

'Plymouth Fury, 1970. Gold.'

'Uh huh. Licence number?'

He told him. Oliver knew he'd be writing it down, old habits.

'So we had the car in the impound and didn't think much of it. Thought someone might claim it or whatever. Tommy's been having some break-ins on the lot lately, so we were set up for a sting anyway, and god-damned did the guy go straight for the same car.'

'He did?'

'First car he went to.'

'So he's holed up somewhere close? He's been cycling through the cars when it's quiet I guess, maybe he saw an old gem like that come in and thought, that's for tonight.'

Oliver leaned against the car and wondered if he'd ever have that kind of instinct. A career's worth.

'We think so. He was squatting in an abandoned house opposite.'

'Alright. So what's troubling you?'

'The guy was waiting, obviously. We know that.'

'We do.'

'But what was he waiting for, would you say? The chance to rob a beat up car driven in on a wrecker? Or the chance to wipe clean some evidence from a stolen car before us country cops figure out what we had?'

'Could be either,' the old man said. 'Could be neither. First thing to do is climb down off the thing and take a look at it.'

'The car?'

Oliver shifted his weight a little where he was leaning on the car and got dust on his shirt.

The old man sighed. 'The situation in its entirety.'

'How do I do that?'

'People, places, facts. Tell me about the guy you got.'

'Caught red handed, as it were. Bag full of tools, broke in through the fence.'

'So he was organised?'

'Not at all. Besides the bag of tools, he was all over the place. Letwin thinks he's slow, you know? Childlike in a way. He can't stop laughing and crying.'

'What about his place?'

'He had a bunch of crap there he'd taken from the cars, nothing of value. Kept asking if he could keep it all.'

'If he's looking to get rid of evidence, why would he stack up a bunch more right across the road? Did he have any cleaning supplies on him? Was he wearing gloves?'

'No, and no.'

'I'd err on the side of coincidence, son. Wrong place, wrong time in my opinion. Unless there's anything I don't know.'

Oliver kneeled to look through the windows of the Fury. Cigarette butts, empty bottles. The glovebox had been rammed closed on a load of papers, maybe a corner of a photograph and bunch of letters, but without the keys all he could do was look. Come midnight the car was on its way out.

'No, I guess not, that's everything,' Oliver said.

'You might be reaching just a little far, son.'

Oliver gripped the phone harder and listened to the soft buzz of the lights above his head.

Seven

Three days into the job and Vince hadn't yet figured out where the cold was coming from. The warehouse was weatherproof with only a few windows, yet every time he stood in the center, looking up at the stars through the skylights, he could feel a breeze on his face as though it came from space itself. In the middle of the night, papers that no one had a use for anymore drifted in the wind with a rustling sound and he never seemed to witness it.

The second night, he'd spread towels and tarps along the bottom of the huge hangar door, then gone and stood in the centre, facing it. The wind was still there.

Why he had to be there every night when nothing was happening, he didn't understand but knew better than to ask. Appearances maybe, in case anyone cared to check a warehouse at four in the morning. Anyone with a badge. Or maybe it was a test. They were testing him for what might be to come. He just did what he was told and took the envelope at the end of it. That was the way to get up, get on to better jobs.

The boss had told him, *bring a book or something, they're gonna be long nights Vinny.*

No one had called him Vinny since baby school but he didn't say nothing about it.

All he had was a set of plastic garden furniture off to one side, under the catwalk. There had been an old CRT TV on wheels in the old office upstairs but he couldn't get it working and he'd eventually pushed it off the catwalk in a rage. An hour of sweeping glass and parts into a corner with his feet.

Tonight was the delivery though. The transporter was due at 1:27am and one of the vehicles was going to have the packages in the back.

All you've got to do is wait for the driver to leave, open it up, call me if anything ain't right. Call Leo if it is. Then lock it back up and you can go home.

No, truckers pick up and drop off all over the country, they couldn't give a shit, they just want to meet their times so they get their bonuses.

Why would they look? Would you look? Vinny? Would you?

He was pacing the catwalk, looking out of each of the high windows in turn when he saw the transporter waiting at the fence. He hadn't honked or anything. Maybe the driver already knew what was up.

The ladder down to the floor was rickety and Vince took it too fast and almost fell.

'I was about to call someone but then I realised you guys never left a number,' the transporter driver shouted down out of his window.

'Yeah,' Vince replied, getting the padlock off the fence and swinging the gate open. It combed the dead leaves on the ground into a neat quarter circle.

The driver had talent or experience, probably both. He turned and backed the transporter up through the hangar doors easily without being guided in.

Vince was eyeing the van on the lower level of the transporter directly behind the cab, wondering if the driver knew about the cargo. Surely he'd have to, but he wasn't saying shit.

'You might as well take a seat for a few,' the driver said as he lowered the ramps. 'Usually we do them in order of delivery but I got a call about an extra vehicle they wanted me to get, so I'll have to shift them around.'

He reversed a pickup truck that looked brand-new off first and parked it at the back of the warehouse. Then a battered looking gold Plymouth Fury with squeaky brakes. He stood looking at that for just a moment or two.

'Don't see those around too often huh?' Vince called over. What he meant was *move along now*.

'Picked it up from the cops, couldn't wait 'til morning, my boss says.'

Vince just stared at him, translating what the man had said. Combing his words for a threat. He could just be stupid, or he could have meant something.

If there's any trouble, which is unlikely, then it's because the driver is a good-old boy and he wants to make trouble. Deal with it as it comes, do I need to write it down for you Vinny?

He stood next to the Fury with his hand in his jacket. He could smell the fumes coming from the exhaust. The driver got out and edged along the side of the transporter, being careful where he put his feet. He hauled himself up into the van. It was the one, Vince knew the licence number.

The driver backed it off fine, lined it up and got out. Nothing went awry until he killed the engine and stepped out.

A thump from the back of the van, unmistakable.

Vince looked at the driver, his eyes. A few seconds passed while he kept his hand in his pocket. He saw the driver's eyes flicker to it.

'Things…sometimes shift around because of the ramps,' the driver said.

Vince nodded. 'I'd imagine.'

The driver raised his eyebrows and shifted his weight.

A minute later they shook hands and the driver walked away with an envelope. Vince watched him load the Fury back onto the transporter and when he got out the envelope didn't get out with him. He loaded the Pickup on behind, rushing it.

Vince watched him drive out, padlocked the gates and shut the hangar doors. Initiative. That's what it was called. He could think on his feet without being told and resolve a hiccup before it became a problem. He'd be reimbursed.

The van looked totally out of place in the middle of all the empty space. He took the keys the driver had given him and went around back.

Deathly silence as he unlocked the door, a stench when it opened.

'What the fuck was that?' he said into the darkness. He didn't know if they knew the words but they got the message at least.

Vince took his phone out, hesitated, then dialed.

Eight

A long time ago they'd sipped wine while the garden got darker and darker around them both. The tealight on the patio table was some unknown sun, and everything beyond it was emptiness, but for the two of them.

She'd said to him that his job was dangerous, and if he ever felt in danger, he should call her and let her know. She'd want to know. It wouldn't be a burden. Yes, even in the middle of the night.

He blocked the light from his phone until he could turn the brightness down. No cars were passing next to him. No other lights and two clear miles ahead on the highway. He would have stood out like a beacon if anyone cared to look. He thought that tonight they may.

He checked the mirrors while the phone rang, nothing following. He was wondering how quick he could really run with all the vehicles on the back, if push came to shove. An image of his entire truck tipping in the grey night and leaving the brand-new Ford and that vintage looking Fury upside down in the road.

'Tony?' Sharp and alert. Maybe this was the night she'd always dreaded.

Or always been waiting for, he thought.

'Yeah it's me. Sorry to wake you.'

'What's going on?'

He told her everything apart from the envelope.

She asked him if he called the police and he said he had. They agreed to keep talking until they arrived. She had work in the morning but neither of them really cared all that much about it.

'How many people?' she asked him. It was getting cold in the truck now, where his coat didn't cover his legs.

'I don't know. I just heard the one noise I think.'

'You think?'

'I heard something that could've been movement when they were loading it up at the depot yesterday, but I didn't think anything of it.'

'Now you do?'

'Now I do. And Ken calls this morning, extra vehicle I need to pick up that just can't wait, but when I get there it's some old car.'

'You think he had a gun?' He can tell her mind is wandering to the worst.

'The guy? Yeah.'

'But you didn't see it?'

'He held it in his jacket but I'm pretty sure.'

'Jesus Christ. He could have shot you.'

'Well that's why I made out like nothing was wrong.'

'That was the right thing to do,' she said. 'That was the right thing.'

A mile down the empty highway, he saw two cars with blue lights. No sirens yet, maybe they wouldn't want to warn the guy.

'I can see them coming.'

Silence for a moment.

'Who?'

'The cops.'

'Oh. Good, good. Just stay there then. Let them come to you.'

'I don't know if they'll arrest me.'

'Why would they?'

He thought about telling her exactly why, but he didn't. 'Well it was, they were on my truck, I loaded it up.'

'You didn't know.'

'I-'

'You didn't, did you?'

'No. I don't know.'

He heard her exhale, pictured her sitting up in bed in the dark. There was a painting above their bed, a balcony looking out over a tiny Mediterranean village where the houses sat on the seashore warming themselves in the sun. He wished he was there.

'No, or you're not sure?' she said.

'No, I didn't know. I didn't.'

He was thinking about the envelope, hidden under the seat of the Fury.

They'd let him drive away after he told them what he knew. Surely they would.

'Is everything okay?'

The blue lights were drawing up, it was actually three cars. Two of them stayed on course and sped past him, the other slowed and turned in the road to pull in behind him.

'I've got to go, the cops are here,' he said.

'OK, let me k-'
He hung up and buried his head in his hands.

Nine

That itch again, stronger this time, telling him to get up and out, breathe some fresh air. He excused himself, saw a couple of the locals roll their eyes without trying to conceal it.

The guy in the hot-seat had said nothing so far, but he'd still managed to bag himself a cigarette.

'If you could find a way to hurry back, Agent Cobb, we'd sure appreciate it,' one of the older ones said with a smirk.

Well, fuck them, he told himself outside the interview room door. He didn't really feel the defiance.

The blinds on the inside window parted for a moment, Cobb pretended not to notice as he headed for the door.

Outside he found a concrete block to sit on where once there might have been plants. He took some breaths. Mid-morning had shown up and there was a bird in the lot, wandering around, killing time having found itself the first to arrive.

You're not supposed to feel this way.

But I do.

You've had all that training and now you want to give up.

I'm not going to give up.

Just because of one truck.

I'm not going to give up. Leave me alone.

You're not strong enough. Everyone was right.

'Agent Cobb?'

He looked around and the Chief, Letwin, was leaning out of the door.

'Yeah?'

'This is an emergency exit. You're not supposed to use it.'

He stood and held out his hands, as though some logic could be plucked from the air.

'We could use you back inside,' the Chief said. 'This is…we haven't dealt with this before.'

'Just a minute, I need to make a call, if you'll grant me that?' he said, trying to hold himself the right way. How the others did.

The Chief stared into his eyes for a moment and then left him.

They can all see it.

They know you don't know what you're doing here.

Past the squad cars still ticking and cooling from their night drive, one of the officers had reversed each vehicle from the transporter and parked them side by side on the lot. That was the first thing Cobb noticed when he pulled in. Everything was already nothing like they'd found it.

He must have got lost in his thoughts for a while, staring.

'Agent Cobb?' This time the Chief came out, jamming the door open with a small planter that seemed heavier than it looked.

'My guys checked all the vehicles thoroughly and found nothing other than what we told you, alright?' he said. 'If you've got concerns I can un…'

'Nothing should have been touched.'

'The driver did the right thing, he's just your average Joe trucker. Maybe it's different where you come from, but here, not everyone's out to get each other. He was trying to do right. He told us where he'd put the money. He took it to save his own skin, I'd have done the same.'

'Where did the rest of it come from? The…papers your officer was talking about?' Cobb asked.

'They were in the glovebox. We didn't know about them before.'

'You held the car almost two days and didn't think to search it?'

'We had no cause to turn someone's car inside out, really.'

'Now you sure do.' Cobb turned away towards the vehicles.

There was a classic car parked on the very end of the row, a brownish gold in colour and looking like it had been through better times. Hardly a collector's item.

'Agent, we've got a man in there we caught with the truck door wide open, full of…you saw it, but it seems you're more interested in some old trash that we don't even know is genuine than the guy we've got sitting in there, who we caught dead to rights, I don't understand it.'

'You wouldn't,' he said.

The chief seemed to chew on something for a second, before swallowing it. They both took a breath and stared in different directions.

'What is it about that fucking car?' the Chief said, staring at the gold vehicle.

He stood for a moment looking across the lot, then turned and went back through the open door.

Off to one side, Cobb saw movement in a window again.

See, they know you can't do this.

He watched a car slow across the road, then speed up.

Ten

Diane had been rearranging stock for three hours, starting the morning by freshening up displays and marking down old items. The window was full of bargains. *New designs, old prices*, a vivid homemade banner said.

She went to turn the sign on the front door back to '*Open, come on in*' and when she got there she found she hadn't actually turned it to '*Closed*' in the first place.

It was already eleven and no single customer had crossed the threshold.

Maybe they'd seen her through the window, elbow deep in cardboard boxes and hauling display cases around and thought better of disturbing her. That could have been it. Perhaps they'd stood with their hand on the door while she had her back to them, looked at their watch and decided to get a cup of coffee somewhere first.

It descended on her all at once, as it always did. The anger she'd built up at a town full of people ordering great truckloads of plastic shit from all over the globe instead of something she made with passion and took time over. She'd reduced, she'd reinvented, she'd networked. Nothing worked and Christmas wasn't a million miles away now. It was about to get cold.

She stood by the windows looking out, forgetting about the display she hadn't finished setting up. The optimism of an autumn clean, vanished like the flame on a lighter.

Why hadn't she taken the place near the mall with the higher rent but a higher footfall? She shouldn't have been so scared of getting into trouble. She should, for once in her little life, have taken a risk.

This place was no risk. Even the location was the opposite of risk. So much so that people made jokes about it almost every day, and each one hit her like a slap.

'Must be a safe place for a jewellery store huh? Right opposite the copshop?'

The same people made the same arrogant little joke before casting their beady eyes around and slinking out without buying anything. The joke was probably what carried them in. The chance to show how witty they were.

She could see over the road something was going on, there had been noise and movement all morning, pretty rare. Someone had left a great ugly car transporter along one side of the lot and there was a gold junkmobile there that looked like some godawful drug-dealer's car. She'd seen a cop going through it earlier, all but stripping it down, turning out all of its pockets. Then he'd gone off inside in some big hurry.

None of them cops worked a full day to save their lives now. None had ever been over to talk to her about protecting her business. They just squawked on Twitter about the 'community'.

She watched a silver SUV with darkened windows slow right down as it passed, then speed up again. To watch it down the road, she had to lean into the window and she almost lost her balance.

Eleven

'I forget who's here and who ain't,' Judy said. The station door had been flapping like a fly's wing all morning and showed no sign of giving it up. The bureau were here, *whoop de doo,* and no one had been out for a breakfast muffin or to pull a cat out of a tree in hours. Must have been some kind of record.

The phone was ringing so much she thought it might be broken, but every call had to be patched through to Letwin or Oliver, whoever wasn't squeezed into the interview room at the time. Oliver was being precious about every little thing, walking around telling everyone he knew something was up all along.

'We all knew something was up and where did it get us?' she said under her breath.

'I'm sorry?' someone asked her, crowding around like they were at a buffet. There were no sneeze guards or nothing. Letwin had a hotplate in his office though. He thought no one knew about it. Sleeping bag too. Rumours.

'I'm just talking to myself, pay me no mind,' she said. She went on typing, imagining what it would be like in a wonderland where people could stand somewhere other than directly in front of her desk while she was trying to concentrate on doing three things at once.

They started filing out into the back rooms, finally. She stood and went to the window to get some air in the room. As she pushed it open, she saw a man in a thick jacket standing in the lot. He saw her too.

He was next to the gold Plymouth they had sitting there, he'd been looking in it through cupped hands, now he was looking directly at her.

'Oliver?' she shouted.

'Everything alright ma'am?' the bureau agent said. He was standing in the emergency exit, letting the door close on him.

'Yes Agent Cobb, well I think so. There's a man outside, sniffing around the cars you got piled up, he don't look quite right.'

The agent hesitated. 'I'll check it out. Would you mind…uh' he gestured towards the corridor leading to the holding cells. Letwin.

'Course.' She cast one last look out the window and hurried down the hall to the interview room, following the sound of raised voices.

Outside she stopped for a beat, hoping she wasn't about to get torn a new one. Then she straightened up, knocked and tried the door.

Whoever was standing directly in front of it took a bump to the foot and moved out of the way. Letwin was on one side of the table next to an empty seat. She didn't look at the man they had sat across the table.

'Chief, there's a man outside sniffing around the cars you brought in, the bureau agent's gone out there, he wondered if you'd-'

Letwin stood immediately and strode towards her. She hurried back the way she came and went back to watch from the window.

They both heard the crack from outside, and Letwin took off running. The second shot came as Letwin crashed out of the door, leaving it rattling in its frame.

Twelve

The engine was still running and Carlos didn't know what the fuck to do. He and Andre stared out across the road, frozen in the middle of their conversation.

'They shot him,' he said.

They'd watched as a guy in a suit, maybe a Fed, had come out and shouted something at Mikael. He'd already had his hand on his gun, Mikael had just been checking the cars for the envelope, heading for the transporter.

The Fed had shot him point blank, stood over him and shot him again.

They watched as one of the country cops came out running, drawing his own weapon.

'This is bad. We should go,' Andre said.

'No. We have to contain the other guy too.'

'How do we do that now? There is no containing here.'

'The same way. Nothing changes.'

They watched as the country cop reached the Fed. He slapped the gun out of his hand, and when the Fed bent to pick it up, he punched him squarely in the jaw twice.

'Who's side is this man on?' Andre said.

'He's just shot an unarmed man and country boy is not happy,' Carlos said.

Nor was he. Yes, he'd known Mikael for less than a week, but still. It was poor manners to shoot him before he knew he was in a fight.

'Mikael is not unarmed.'

'The Fed didn't know that, did he?'

'If we're not driving away, what are we doing?' Andre said.

They could see Mikael coughing up blood onto the asphalt, flat on his back.

'They are not used to this. We overwhelm them, they'll never expect it. We start with the Fed and country boy, if there are more we'll get to them. Find our guy. This *Vinny.*'

'*If* there's any more? *If?* Have you seen how many cars there are?'

They looked past the three men next to the gold Fury, to a line of squad cars.

'They just park them there. Doesn't mean they're here.'

Without another word, Carlos got out of the car and crossed the road towards Mikael. He saw he'd stopped coughing up blood and was lying still. The country cop was bent over him, his hands were covered with blood. He didn't see them coming.

The Fed picked his gun up off the ground.

'Stop right there, back off!'

'Hey, whoa!' Carlos called out. 'I'm a doctor, I was driving by, perhaps I can help.'

The Chief snarled something at the Fed and his gun dropped just a little, enough.

Carlos watched Andre take his gun from his waistband and did the same with his own.

They each fired four shots, the country cop took two from Carlos and went down straight away, the other two went over his head towards the building.

The Fed had ducked behind the gold car and two of Andre's rounds had passed through a tire and hit him in the small of the back.

Andre and Carlos said nothing to each other and advanced on the station.

Thirteen

'Andre? Hey, Andre?'

'My name is Judy, ask me about my Grandchildren,' Andre said, too quiet to be heard.

'Hey, wake up,' Carlos snapped his fingers in front of Andre's face, then slapped the name badge he was holding out of his hands, it clattered onto the floor in the corner of the office, bringing back a wave of noise.

People were shouting down the corridor, questions and threats or instructions.

Andre turned to look out of the small hole in the spiderwebbed window, then down onto the woman, flat on her back beneath it.

The blow came as he was raising a hand to touch the bullet hole in the glass. Carlos' slap knocked him off balance and into the wall. When he came back to himself, his partner was standing over him with fury in his eyes.

He shook his head, tightened his grip on his gun and checked the magazine.

'Sorry, I'm sorry,' he said.

Carlos could have barely made himself heard, so he just held out his hand.

Andre reached into his jacket pocket and handed over two canisters. Then he moved to the door and poked his head around quickly, the voices roared but he ignored them, he'd seen what he needed to see.

Andre handed Carlos a gas mask and Carlos slipped it onto his head but didn't pull it down. He was still closely watching Andre.

'There are no windows on the west side of the building,' Carlos said, 'I have the South covered from here.'

Andre nodded. 'I'll cover the rest.'

Andre watched Carlos pull his mask down and take the pin from one of the canisters. He tossed it down the corridor. Andre heard it clang against something metal.

Outside, his hands shook as he stood at the corner of the building. The station backed onto woods and he could hear birds chirping back and forth to each other. Warnings, no doubt. A handful of them rose with a flutter and tore off across the sky.

The blinds were down on all four windows he could see. It was unlikely the interview room would have a window, but all exits had to be covered.

He jumped when he heard shots, seven rounds, a gap of a few seconds, four more. Then three more from another weapon.

No movement from any of the windows.

No movement on the road. Their car was waiting for them, he longed for it. He stood with his hands at his sides and wondered if something might be breaking inside him, where it was whole before.

The main doors burst open and Carlos backed out of the door, dragging an unconscious man by his wrists. He dropped a load of papers on the ground, unable to hold everything. The envelope was among them.

'Get the letters, the papers,' Carlos barked through his mask.

Andre rushed to gather them up and help carry the unconscious man. There were photographs among the papers, and a letter written with stencils like a ransom note.

'This is our guy?'

'Ours, yes, Vinny the mob-movie payoff man who puts us all at risk,' Carlos said.

'What about the other guy, the driver?'

'The police released him, we tracked him down a short time after that. He made a call after the meeting with this Vinny. We're tracing it. There is a freelancer tying up loose ends. Those are for him.'

Andre looked down at the papers he was holding. They seemed like nothing.

'It's all there?'

'We had better hope so. We meet him in thirty minutes.' Carlos let go of the man's arms to look for the car keys. Andre crouched down and took a deep breath, leaning against the door of a gold Plymouth Fury.

Carlos found the keys and they dragged Vinny across the empty road to their SUV. Andre opened a rear passenger door. There were cars further down the highway now coming towards them, civilian looking and slowing, but still.

He thought he saw someone in a shop, looking out towards the road.

'We need to hurry,' Andre said.

'What?' Carlos said, looking over his shoulder towards the row of storefronts.

'Nothing, what's the matter?'

'You were looking at something. Did you see someone?'

'No, nobody.' Andre said.

Carlos slammed the door, the man inside now stretched across the seats.

'Carlos?' Andre said as his partner stepped over a hedge and headed for a jewellery store.

'She saw us. Start the car, Andre,' Carlos called back over his shoulder.

Fourteen

Everything rattled. Boxes full of belongings, food, clothes, vibrating together with the engine. Sarah yawned into the back of her hand, glancing at her sleeping friend in the passenger seat.

Ahead, there was movement.

'Hey wake up, something's going down.'

Further down the road, a man was standing by the open door of a silver SUV, watching another man force the door of a jewellery store. His jacket blew slightly in the wind, as though it wanted to drag him away from what he was doing.

Sarah slowed a little, 'look, look, what's he doing?' she said. Her friend was now fully awake and leaning towards the windscreen the better to see.

'I don't like it.'

'No.'

'Can you stop?'

'In the middle of the road? Not really.'

Sarah slowed more, almost to a crawl, about ten car lengths from the SUV. The man next to it had now turned towards them.

'He's looking. Shi-'

A crack like the backfire of a car drew their eyes back to the shop. The glass door shattered and fell to the ground, leaving the shooter free to step over through the doorframe.

Sarah had stopped the car by then, they were idling in no man's land between both lanes. Sarah could feel the weight of all of her friend's belongings stacked behind them, like a wall.

'Shit!'

Sarah hammered the accelerator and the car shot towards the SUV. Both of them saw the man next to it draw a gun from his pocket and aim it, but Sarah couldn't have steered away from the shot in time. It passed through the windscreen, shattering it but leaving the glass in place and impossible to see through. The bullet lodged into the roof between their heads.

She lost control and the wheel slipped away from her. They barreled through the central divide, just a thin, low wooden fence.

The car drove as though it too was trying to escape. It mounted the curb on the wrong side of the road. All four wheels took their turn to leave the ground as it sailed over a small grass verge. The final impact came as it rammed into the side of a red pickup truck.

A breaking wave of shattered safety glass. Scattered beads and crafting materials spread out onto the road. Lying next to one wheel, a bottle of drain cleaner, dented and leaking onto the asphalt. The engine roared and a front wheel spun, burning rubber against the ground.

Her friend was knocked unconscious by the impact but Sarah wasn't. She looked out of her window in a daze, fighting the airbag with shaking arms. She could see the colour gold, the shape of a car came into focus.

There were three bodies on the ground by the gold car and an approaching figure in the rearview mirror before she passed out.

Another crack came from the direction of the shop, and one more.

Nobody saw the pickup truck idling further back down the road, its driver suffering a brief paralysis.

Fifteen

Nicole had three monitors on her desk, scanning social media for anything usable. The station had been on live coverage of the story for over an hour already. A reporter was on the way to the scene, but they were flailing, the report was slowly revolving in the same pattern of information, like a spinning top about to lose balance and topple.

This was what she'd moved for, and now it was here, she was overwhelmed. Almost all the previous night she'd been awake. The new apartment was fine, but it was full of glass furniture she never would have picked.

Yeah they come with the lease. You can move 'em if you want but don't break 'em.

Her own things were still packed away in the spare room.

Nights like that made her wonder if she could make any of it stick. The change, the leap. What her mother called her 'grand gesture' down the phone whenever they spoke.

'Whatever it takes,' she'd said to herself, her voice echoed off the walls. The dead of night.

People in the office were starting to panic about losing ratings. Then she found a video.

She sent a message to the account that had posted it, asking for permission to use it, promising a wire transfer instant payment and the chance to make a difference and maybe catch the guys. Hoping it would be enough. She opened an IM box with the station chief.

Got something.

What?

Dashcam POV of the second half of the police station attack from a pickup that was there but got away I guess. Multiple gunshots, nothing gory so we could show it. Chasing permission now.

Link?

Here.

Holy shit. We need this. Great work. Let me know.

She sat chewing her nails and hitting refresh on her inbox.

'Yes!'

We've got it, they've replied, can you authorize payment with finance?

Yeah. Let's get it up as quickly as possible. Exclusivity?

I'll do my best, I'll offer more money, he may have already approached other channels.

Whatever it takes, Nicole.

Ten minutes later, almost the entire station stood around the largest monitor as the on-the-scene reporter talked to the camera.

In the background was the police parking lot, where the blue car from the video was visible, the front end crushed. Next to it and half out of frame, a vehicle that looked older, gold or brown in colour. Ambulance lights were pulsing behind it, and there were people in white coveralls and reflective jackets out of focus.

The boss looked over to Nicole and nodded as the reporter introduced the footage, making sure to warn viewers it was disturbing. She clenched her fists at her sides in triumph.

Dashcam footage from a pickup.

Blue car stopping in the road.

Gunshots out of frame.

The car swerving off the road.

A man approaching, checking a magazine.

Three more shots.

'Shit shit, oh my God, fuck!' a voice on the dashcam said. The footage blurred as the driver swung the pickup around.

The crowd around the monitor stood silent for a moment. Several of Nicole's colleagues turned to look at her.

Sixteen

The dog had been loose an hour and he wasn't barking. Probably meant he was up to something he shouldn't be. Harley leaned on his stick and wrenched the back door open onto a good sunset.

'Squirrel chasing weather.'

'Buck!' he hollered out into the garden. He'd be down there in the ditch somewhere, but Harley's days of going after him were over. He'd come back when he got hungry. The dog was as dumb as a post but he knew where his food bowl was.

He left the door ajar enough to be nosed open and went back to his chair in front of the TV. What Oliver had said to him had been playing on his mind since the call, as though it was his own case. He never slept a night's worth anyway.

'You're a tired old man, that's all,' he said to himself as he watched the news.

It couldn't be. He was just seeing what he wanted to see. Maybe he needed something to look into like he needed his pills or his supplements.

No, hold your horses.

His notebook was still on the table where he left it. He paused the TV, making sure to catch it on just the right frame for what he needed, and struggled up again.

'Buck!' he shouted from the door. No dog came running.

Notebook in hand, he sat back down and scanned through, then looked up at the TV.

'Well god damn. Maybe I ain't quite crazy yet, even if I'm expected shortly.'

It was the same car. Gold Plymouth Fury, next to a blue saloon that had T-boned a pickup. Same licence number.

'Where the hell is this anyway?' he said. He went back to the live feed, catching a reporter on the scene signing off.

'Jesus Christ,' he said, and leaned over for his phone. His hands shook and he couldn't get the numbers in the right order.

'Goddamn piece of shit.'

He took it slow and got it right.

A dial tone, three, four rings.

A clatter from outside and the old man froze in his seat. The back door burst open and Buck barged his way past the dining room chairs and sat by his side, panting.

The phone kept ringing and ringing.

'He was right,' the old man said. 'Oliver was right and I was wrong. It wasn't no coincidence. Oliver pick up. Pick up.'

Still the phone rang.

Seventeen

He couldn't sleep for the beeps, the endless beeps like tiny holes being bored into his head all night. When morning rolled around again he asked to be moved somewhere else but they wouldn't let him, they said they had no other rooms but he knew that was a lie.

He'd asked a nurse if there were police guarding his room and hadn't got a straight answer.

From the window by his bed he could see the entrance. He watched cars and ambulances coming and going, visitors, nurses, doctors. This was the longest he'd ever been in one room in his life. He had to watch police arrive, then lie there waiting for them to make their way through the building and come in again. Go over the same thing. Listen to them blame him for being the victim of a random carjacking instead of finding the person who did it to him.

He should have known, of course he should, that this was the direction things would go. No one gets an opportunity like he'd had without it being ripped away again. Well, people like him didn't anyway. Normal people who work for a living.

The theater's hiring. They want guys to unload equipment and pack it away again after shows. You could do that.

Sure, he could do that, if that's all Jess thought he was worth. He would have told her where to shove it but they, he, needed the money. At least he could take his camera, his real work. Maybe get a few shots of the empty theater after hours. Anyone famous who rolled through.

Turns out he'd been a little too good at the job, surprise surprise. Finished loading away the PA system in record time after some bullshit rally, gone midnight. Followed the sound of voices to a bus with blacked out windows.

They hadn't seen him. He heard it, first of all. They thought there was no one around. No one in the driver's seat.

He knew he was right to keep bringing his camera, day-in, day-out.

They never heard the shutter clicking. God it was awful, but that was good, all the better. He took his opportunity from the stairs at the front of the bus and then got out clean. Quit the job the very next day. Wouldn't be needing it. He only needed to write a letter.

Maher came back to himself as the door to his room opened. This one looked different. Not local. More senior. Calm as he walked in.

They told me I was dangerously dehydrated and in the early stages of hypothermia when they found me collapsed under a hedge. All night I'd been there.

Well I got all turned around.

The guy told me to run and not to look back, and he had a gun.

By the time I was sure he'd gone it was getting dark. I wasn't sure where the road even was.

No, I couldn't hear anything.

The truth was, he'd been petrified. He didn't want to get shot. So yeah, he hid, and that was his business. He had no need to ever say it out loud. He'd lost everything, he wasn't about to lose his privacy now too. Even if he used it to be a coward.

It was karma, he knew it now. He'd tried to take what he knew and make some money, enough to get out of everything and start again. Then fate had pulled a gun on him and all hope had driven off without him.

Yes, that's all I know. I already told you what he looked like.

I don't care what you say about it, that's how he looked. I'm not making it up.

They wanted him to look at pictures now.

Of what?

What car? My car?

Stop calling me Daniel like you know me, would you please? It's Mr Maher. Yes, that's my car, a gold Plymouth Fury, 1970.

Yeah, great so he totalled it? Fantastic. Yes, the licence matches, that's my car. I told you.

Why are you asking me about what was in it?

How is it relevant to the investigation? I'm the victim, you had no right to…

I can't see that, I need my glasses…OK, yeah that's my handwriting.

Well why would you be looking though my letters? It's my personal property that had nothing to do with what happened.

What 'reasons' do you have to suspect a crime has been committed?

I wasn't trying to blackmail anyone.

No, I'm not looking at anything else. I've got no further comments.

So what if it was sealed? You had no right to open it.

How fucking dare you? I will sue you for invasion of privacy, I hope you know that.

I want a lawyer. Arrest me or get out.

You wouldn't dare talk to her. She has nothing to do with anything. Leave her alone.

Get off me, what is that?

Hey?! I said what is…

What is th…

Eighteen

After he washed the hospital smell from his skin, he threw away the suit he'd been wearing and stood looking out of his motel room window onto a flat concrete wall on the other side. A TV shouted through the walls about something that wasn't important.

The twitch in his face was returning. Fatigue or irritation.

The client's chasers had done well, a lot of the mess was contained even after the scene they'd created at the police station. Yes, the situation had bled more than was ideal, but they'd managed to get a tourniquet on it eventually. They'd even found the letters and the cash.

That should have been a minimum requirement of course, but this wasn't his organisation and he often found he had to realign his expectations of his clients' people. All the more reason to stay freelance.

He'd only had two calls to make so far, now a final call and the job would be done

He laid out each of the letters on the bed in date order. Several old drafts of the same empty threats and impossible demands. He also had the original, the one Maher had sent direct to the client. It was a clumsy attempt, even after all the drafting.

Among the letters were photographs, poorly lit, but devastating none the less. Their existence was clearly avoidable. Again, not his organisation.

At first he'd questioned whether the carjacking had even happened. His natural suspicion grasped for the missing complication, the unseen cleverness of Maher, an underlying plan. He'd ultimately come up dry and concluded the man had been as simple and hopeless as he'd seemed.

Among the leverage documents Maher had kept with him, his 'insurance policy' as he had so ham-handedly called them, were a few unrelated letters Maher had received from a loanshark. Dated from the previous spring and through the winter. The temperature of wording changed along with the date. Maher had kept them hidden too.

He turned them over on the bed as he read them. His back twinging each time he leaned down.

There were also insurance documents for a gold 1970 Plymouth Fury, that had expired months before. The chasers had recovered it all from the police station, the only reason they were still able to walk, as his client had inferred. The operation had been productive if not quiet. One of them seemed immensely proud to have taken the papers from a table right in the middle of a room full of 'slumbering' cops. Funny turn of phrase on him. Some kind of foreign.

Many mistakes had been made. The photographs were damning. Even he barely wanted to look at them. The client would want to dispose of them himself when matters were settled. Though, of course, he would keep copies for his archives, as always.

He moved the papers from the bed and sat down. His back was giving him hell and the day was not yet over.

Daniel Maher had received no visitors since they found him. His wife had stayed at home virtually the whole time. They'd kept an eye on her but had been unable to make a move in case she was being guarded. Unnecessary precaution, as it turned out.

Mrs Maher had called the nurses for updates on dear Daniel but asked them not to tell him about it.

Maher had never sent her the final letter, the one that had been sealed until some local cop saw fit to open it. She wouldn't even know it existed.

Jess,

I'm so sorry for how things have been. It's my fault. There's things that you don't know, that hopefully you'll never have to know. You deserve better than me, so I'm going to leave. I'm weighing you down and it's not worth it for you.

I'll be gone by the time you read this. I'm taking the car, not that it's of any value, but I won't take anything else.

Pretend you never knew me, until it feels like you didn't.

Love, Dan.

What a shitty way to bail out on someone. And he hadn't even had the guts to send it. Just left her in the lurch. What a mouse.

Maybe the carjacking had been karma, or something like it.

It wasn't just how the letter was written, but how it said so little. Maher was hiding something more than his debt from her.

Two birds with one stone, he must have hoped. Blow town with a bunch of blackmail money, get rid of the old ball and chain at the same time.

Maybe he should let her know about who her husband really was. Since he'd be visiting anyway.

He got up to head out, stopping for second, deciding on something. Then he walked back to the drawer, took out a clean tie and held it against himself in front of the mirror and smiled twice, three times, until it looked right.

Nineteen

She'd been watching the news like everyone else. Sitting in the living room in that constant state of limbo. Should she go to the hospital or not? Was it the right thing to do, or the stupid thing to do?

How he could have got so far into debt she'd never know. She'd turned the house upside down and found no trace of it. What had he used any of that money for?

The policeman, Oliver, had told her his debt was up to a hundred thousand. None of it looked to be secured against the house, but Daniel's Plymouth Fury was a different story.

She'd laughed then and told him she didn't care about her husband's car. Not one little bit. She didn't know anything about any loansharks.

'Other than the debt, would you have any reason to think there was something he was involved in?' Oliver had asked her. He'd kept squeezing one of his hands into a ball, over and over.

'How do you mean?'

'Did you get the impression he was hiding anything else from you?'

'Well…no. Did you? Do you know something?'

He'd paused for a second and then told her that no, he didn't know anything else. She could tell he was lying, but she had no energy left to push it. It was just another lying man, after all.

Then he'd got up and left, limping. She didn't ask. He seemed awfully sad.

She watched him from the window as he sat back in his car. He didn't drive away immediately.

Now she sits in the same chair barely seeing the TV screen in front of her until something breaks through. A flash of a familiar colour. A shine of gold, a shape she knows. She pauses, leans in, reads the numbers.

What now? What else? They told her it was found in a field, not crashed in some parking lot.

She doesn't get to hear the rest of the story.

Three knocks interrupt it and she wonders whether to answer at all, staying in the living room where she can't be seen from the door.

The man at the door smiles sadly at her, oddly, even.

He apologises for the intrusion. Yet another shirt and tie, another pair of ears for yet another set of questions. He has a slow, calm way about him. It makes her want to shrug her shoulders. He follows her inside.

They sit across from each other at the dining room table. There are photographs of Daniel and Jess together at the fair in a frame on the wall. Light from the afternoon sun is stretched out across the floor.

The neighbourhood is quiet. Some way off, a car door closes, somebody calls out, then again.

He asks if she had any idea what her husband had found himself in the middle of.

'The debts? No I had no idea. I'm still trying to figure out–'

He shakes his head and it stops her mid-sentence. He wants to give her some information.

'The other police didn't make it sound like there was any more to it, but I knew there was,' she says.

He lays three photographs on the desk, face down. Turns the first over slowly.

He says he wonders if she recognises any of the men in the photograph.

She narrows her eyes, hoping to recognise them. Needing for things to make sense, but it doesn't.

'Sorry, no,' she says.

He shrugs and turns over the second.

Again she wishes, but nothing gets any clearer, the opposite in fact as she wonders what Daniel's blundered into, how much she doesn't know.

She shakes her head.

He smiles and brushes the first two photographs off the table into his hand.

'Wait, what are those?' She says, pointing to another pile of papers. Letters, it looks like.

He tells her it's nothing, he'll get to that.

'Okay.' Her heart is thudding and she doesn't know quite why.

Her phone rings, buzzing on the table, the hospital.

He places a palm over the phone and smiles. Asking for a little longer. A little more of her time.

She nods and silences her phone. Within seconds it rings again and they both look at it until the display turns off.

He turns over the final photograph. She leans in to look at it.

Her heart leaps with the sense of an answer. She taps the photograph as she speaks.

'That's the guy from the TV! I've seen his campaign ad. What the hell does Daniel have to do with him?' She almost smiles because it's so ridiculous. 'John Mandle, that's his name. Oh my God, what is he…why are you showing me that? That's disgusting.'

He takes a slow breath.

The landline begins ringing in the kitchen.

'Someone really needs to get hold of me,' she says, putting her hands on the table to get up.

He raises a palm, keeps her eye contact, moves his hand downwards, index finger extended.

There's a pause.

'What did you say your name was, officer?'

He begins to sweep some more of his papers off the table into a pile.

'I want to know,' she says. She's shaking now. 'I want to see your ID, your badge, please.'

He shakes his head, dismissive. It's time for the other papers.

He slides them to her face down.

She doesn't want to look at them, she knows it must be bad, it must be Daniel.

He stares at her until she turns one over. She doesn't read it right away, she looks everywhere but the letter.

He tells her to look at it.

It's addressed to her, from Daniel.

Her eyes fill with tears, she wants to throw up, or pass out.

Somewhere in her mind, things fall into place, before she sees him reach into his jacket pocket.

Twenty

He snips the landline cable in the kitchen, so that it doesn't ring endlessly and alert the neighbours in the night. Then, he pockets the rest of the photographs and letters. He leaves Maher's letter on the table and lays the gun on the floor by Mrs Maher's hand. Kind of her to turn her head, at the last moment. Mandle will fix the finer details, if there's any interest.

He likes to play a game most times. It's all about wondering whether things could have been different. Imagining his way out of his own work. It's almost like therapy, not that he needs such a thing.

If she hadn't identified Mandle? If she'd shrugged and been stupid, would she be where she was now?

Probably she would. She all but confirmed she had no idea about Mandle beforehand. Her husband hadn't passed any information to her. Seemed like that was his way. But the client had insisted, so there wasn't much manoeuvring room on this one. Not the most fun game he'd ever played. Not the most fun job, either.

Her phone rings again, he reads the screen then leaves it on the table.

Somewhere outside, a car crawls past. A child shouts or sings. Then quiet again.

He takes a breath, steps over her, undoing his tie as he goes. It was choking him.

On his way to the door, he passes the TV. He only glances for a moment at the dashcam footage on screen and it means nothing to him. Years ago he would have connected it. Seen the web spreading out of his control, not yet swept away.

Outside, the afternoon sun is still bright, but it's cold. It's a strange kind of light, he thinks to himself as he gets into the car. Like it could be winter, or summer, or the surface of mars.

THANK YOU

If you've enjoyed Gold Fury, please consider adding a review on Amazon and Goodreads and recommending it to your friends.

I also have a creative writing YouTube channel at

youtube.com/kierenwestwoodwriting

Made in the USA
Middletown, DE
11 October 2023